PRINCESS K.I.M.

and the lie that grew

By MARYANN COCCA-LEFFLER

Albert Whitman & Company
Morton Grove, Illinois

Library of Congress Cataloging-in-Publication Data

Cocca-Leffler, Maryann, 1958-
Princess K.I.M. and the lie that grew / by Maryann Cocca-Leffler.
p. cm.
Summary: After new girl Kim tells her classmates she is from
a royal family, her lie grows and grows.
ISBN 978-0-8075-4178-4
[1. Honesty–Fiction. 2. Self-acceptance–Fiction. 3. Schools–Fiction.]
I. Title. II. Title: Princess Kim and the lie that grew.
PZ7.C638Pr 2009 [E]–dc22 2008028056

10 9 8 7 6 5 4 3 2 1

Type design by Jill Weber.

For more information about Albert Whitman,
please visit our web site at www.albertwhitman.com.

Please visit Maryann at her web site, www.maryanncoccaleffler.com.

Jill–thanks for all your help.–M.C.-L.

To Collin—
You will always
be a prince to me.
Love,
Maryann

It was Kim's first day of school in a new town. New school. New friends. Kim was nervous. "What if the kids don't like me?" she said.

"They will love you, my princess," said her dad. "Just be your charming self."

Kim's teacher, Mrs. Della, ushered Kim to the front of the room.

"Class, I want to introduce our new student."

The other children stopped and stared.

"This is Kim Worthington," Mrs. Della said.

"Not another Kim!" called a girl from the back. "My name is Kim!"

All the kids laughed.

"Oh, no," Kim thought. "I have to make them like me!"

So in a tiny voice, Kim told a teeny, tiny, bitty lie . . .

"My name is not Kim.

It's K. I. M.

It stands for

Katherine Isabella Marguerite."

"Very pretty," said the teacher. "That sounds like the name of a queen."

Kim stood up straight, and out of her mouth came another teeny, tiny lie.

"I come from a royal family, you know."

"Oh, I didn't know."

The teacher smiled and bowed a long, low bow.

"Welcome to our school, Katherine Isabella Marguerite Worthington," she said.

All the kids saw the teacher bow. Soon word got out.

"The new girl, Katherine Isabella Marguerite, is from royalty!"

Later that day the kids swarmed around "Katherine."
They all wanted to be her friend. Kim loved the attention.
Her teeny, tiny lie got bigger....

"I am a princess.

My grandmother is a queen."

"Can you believe it? A princess in our school!" said Abby.

"I don't believe it," Jason said.

"Princesses don't live in Greenville."

The next day, on Tuesday, Jason and Abby watched as a man walked Katherine to school. He held an umbrella over her head. As he handed over her lunch bag, they heard him call her "Princess."

"See, I told you! That must be her butler!" said Abby.

Jason rolled his eyes. "Oh, sure!"

"After you."

"I would be happy to give you my lunch."

All that day, and the next, Katherine was treated like royalty.

"Watch your step."

"I'll carry that!"

On Thursday, Katherine took the bus to school. She wore the golden tiara from her dance recital. Then she put on the fancy ring she won at the arcade. Her teeny, tiny lie got bigger and BIGGER . . .

"This ring is from the queen herself.

My crown
is made
of
real
diamonds!"

On Friday, Katherine was mobbed as soon as she got off the bus.

"Will you take a picture with me?"

"Can I have your autograph?"

Everyone seemed impressed except Jason. He walked by, tossing a baseball in the air.

Just then Abby slipped Katherine an invitation. "Princess Katherine, I would be honored if you would come to my birthday party this weekend," Abby said. Without thinking, Katherine-Kim-replied, "I can't. My grandmother is coming to visit."

Abby screamed, "Your grandmother—THE QUEEN!?"

Kim gulped. "Oops!"

The kids came running over.

"Can we meet her?" asked Sandy.

"Does she have a royal carriage?" asked Kevin.

"We want to meet the queen!" the kids chanted.

Kim didn't know what to say. Her teeny, tiny lie had grown into a **big fat giant problem.** And she couldn't stop the lie from growing.

Each time the lie was passed along, it got **BIGGER and BIGGER.**

The queen is visiting Greenville this weekend!"

By the end of the day, the news was out.

Kim was glad to be going home.

On Saturday, when Grandma Betty came to pick her up, Kim gladly left her crown at home.

They went to Kim's ballet class and then out for ice cream.

On Sunday, they spent all day at the zoo.

Kim almost forgot about her big fat giant problem, until that evening.

"Time for bed, Kim. There's school tomorrow!" Grandma Betty called. "Good night, my princess."

"I'm not a princess!" said Kim. And she began to cry.

"What's the matter?" asked Grandma Betty.

Kim told her the whole story.

Grandma Betty listened hard, then said, "That *is* quite a problem. But things will look brighter in the morning."

Kim was not so sure.

On Monday, as soon as Kim got on the bus, the kids started yelling at her.

"We watched you all weekend! We didn't see the queen," said Sandy.

"We didn't see a royal carriage, either!" said Kevin.

"All we saw was an old lady and a Buick," said Abby.

"Princess Katherine Isabella Marguerite—you are a FAKE!"

Kim sank in her seat. The weight of
her crown grew heavy.
Finally the bus pulled up to the school.
Kim felt even worse when she saw a large
crowd waiting.

Kim slowly got off the bus.

She couldn't believe her eyes!
There at the curb was a big shiny
car. Everyone watched as a man in a
black suit rolled out a red carpet.
He opened the car door and stood back.

A silver shoe poked out.

The children glimpsed a sparkling emerald-green dress,

then a long purple cape,

and finally, a golden crown.

An elegant lady stepped gracefully from the car.

It was Kim's grandmother . . .

the QUEEN!

"My princess, you forgot your lunch."
The stunned students stood in silence.
They parted to let the queen and princess
go by.

"Allow me to escort you to your classroom,
my dear princess," said the queen.

Kim took the queen's hand, and they started walking up the red carpet.

Suddenly Kim stopped. She couldn't stand it anymore. Out of her mouth came the **big fat truth.**

'My name

"is not Princess Katherine Isabella Marguerite. My name is Kim. Just plain Kim."

Kim handed her crown to Grandma Betty. "You will always be a princess to me," whispered her grandmother.

That day, no one paid attention to Kim.
No one offered to open doors
or carry her backpack.

But Kim was happy.
Without the crown, she was
free to be herself.

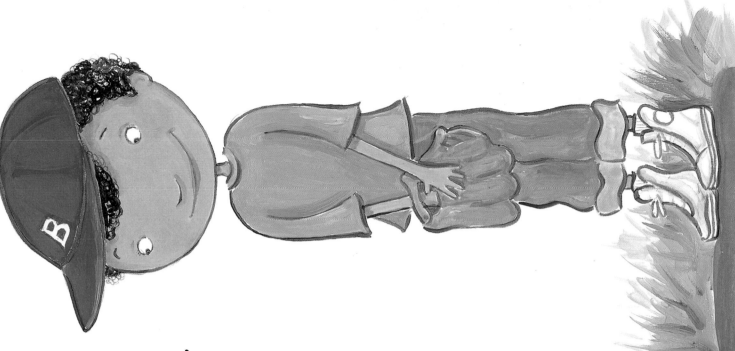

At recess, Kim sat on the grass and read her book.
A ball rolled to her feet. She looked up. Jason was standing there.

"Want to play catch?" he asked.

"ME?" Kim was surprised. "In case you haven't heard, I'm not a princess or anything. I'm just plain Kim."

"Oh–I knew it all along!" Jason said. "Last year, I told everyone my dad owned the Red Sox!"

"OH?" said Kim.

"Plus, I like just plain Kim," said Jason.

"Me, too!" said Kim.

"Catch!"